CHILDREN'S THRIFT CLASSICS

Sleeping Beauty and Other Fairy Tales

JACOB AND WILHELM GRIMM

*Illustrated by Harriet Golden
and Thea Kliros*

DOVER PUBLICATIONS, INC.
New York

DOVER CHILDREN'S THRIFT CLASSICS
EDITOR: PHILIP SMITH

Published in Canada by General Publishing Company, Ltd., 30 Lesmill Road, Don Mills, Toronto, Ontario.

Published in the United Kingdom by Constable and Company, Ltd., 3 The Lanchesters, 162–164 Fulham Palace Road, London W6 9ER.

This Dover edition, first published in 1992, is a new selection of unabridged tales from *Household Stories, from the Collection of the Bros. Grimm,* translated by Lucy Crane, originally published by Macmillan and Company, New York, in 1886. An introductory note and illustrations have been specially prepared for this edition.

Manufactured in the United States of America
Dover Publications, Inc., 31 East 2nd Street, Mineola, N.Y. 11501

Library of Congress Cataloging-in-Publication Data

Grimm, Jacob, 1785–1863.
    Sleeping Beauty and other fairy tales / Jacob and Wilhelm Grimm ; illustrated by Harriet Golden.
        p.   cm. — (Dover children's thrift classics)
    Summary: Includes ten traditional fairy tales in their unabridged versions.
    ISBN 0-486-27084-X (pbk.)
    1. Fairy tales—Germany. [1. Fairy tales. 2. Folklore—Germany.] I. Grimm, Wilhelm, 1786–1859. II. Golden, Harriet, ill. III. Title. IV. Series.
PZ8.G882Slc 1992
398.21'0943—dc20
                              91–39703
                              CIP
                              AC

Note

The stories in this volume have been popular with children around the world for hundreds of years. Originally folk-tales that were spread and adapted without being written down, these stories were given their present form by two German brothers, Jacob (1785–1863) and Wilhelm (1786–1859) Grimm. The Brothers Grimm gathered their tales from many sources, including local peasantry, and wrote them down, adding details of their own invention (often in imitation of the styles of native storytellers).

Wildly successful from their first appearance, the fairy tales of the Brothers Grimm have been translated into dozens of languages and have become a part of the spoken culture of regions far from the Brothers' Europe. This volume contains English translations of the tales that were done soon after the Grimms' time. They contain many details struck from later versions, details that give the stories much of their flavor and mystery.

Contents

List of Illustrations

*Illustration by Thea Kliros.

Sleeping Beauty

IN TIMES PAST there lived a king and queen, who said to each other every day of their lives, "Would that we had a child!" and yet they had none. But it happened once that when the queen was bathing, there came a frog out of the water, and he squatted on the ground, and said to her,

"Thy wish shall be fulfilled; before a year has gone by, thou shalt bring a daughter into the world."

And as the frog foretold, so it happened; and the queen bore a daughter so beautiful that the king could not contain himself for joy, and he ordained a great feast. Not only did he bid to it his relations, friends, and acquaintances, but also the wise women, that they might be kind and favourable to the child. There were thirteen of them in his kingdom, but as he had only provided twelve golden plates for them to eat from, one of them had to be left out. However, the feast was celebrated with all splendour; and as it drew

1

to an end, the wise women stood forward to present to the child their wonderful gifts: one bestowed virtue, one beauty, a third riches, and so on, whatever there is in the world to wish for. And when eleven of them had said their say, in came the uninvited thirteenth, burning to revenge herself, and without greeting or respect, she cried with a loud voice,

"In the fifteenth year of her age the princess shall prick herself with a spindle and shall fall down dead."

And without speaking one more word she turned away and left the hall. Every one was terrified at her saying, when the twelfth came forward, for she had not yet bestowed her gift, and though she could not do away with the evil prophecy, yet she could soften it, so she said,

"The princess shall not die, but fall into a deep sleep for a hundred years."

Now the king, being desirous of saving his child even from this misfortune, gave commandment that all the spindles in his kingdom should be burnt up.

The maiden grew up, adorned with all the gifts of the wise women; and she was so lovely, modest, sweet, and kind and clever, that no one who saw her could help loving her.

It happened one day, she being already fifteen years old, that the king and queen rode abroad, and the maiden was left behind alone in the castle. She wandered about into all the nooks and corners, and into all the chambers and parlours, as the fancy took her, till at last she came to an old tower. She climbed the narrow winding stair which led to a little door, with a rusty key sticking out of the lock; she turned the key, and the door opened, and there in the little room sat an old woman with a spindle, diligently spinning her flax.

"Good day, mother," said the princess, "what are you doing?"

"I am spinning," answered the old woman, nodding her head.

"What thing is that that twists round so briskly?" asked the maiden, and taking the spindle into her hand she began to spin; but no sooner had she touched it than the evil prophecy was fulfilled, and she pricked her finger with it. In that very moment she fell back upon the bed that stood there, and lay in a deep sleep. And this sleep fell upon the whole castle: the king and queen, who had returned and were in the great hall, fell fast asleep, and with them the whole court. The horses in their stalls, the dogs in the yard, the pigeons on the roof, the flies on the wall, the very fire that flickered on the hearth, became still, and slept like the rest; and the meat on the spit ceased roasting, and the cook, who was going to pull the scullion's hair for some mistake he had made, let him go, and went to sleep. And the wind ceased, and not a leaf fell from the trees about the castle.

Then round about that place there grew a hedge of thorns thicker every year, until at last the whole castle was hidden from view, and nothing of it could be seen but the vane on the roof. And a rumour went abroad in all that country of the beautiful sleeping Rosamond, for so was the princess called; and from time to time many kings' sons came and tried to force their way through the hedge; but it was impossible for them to do so, for the thorns held fast together like strong hands, and the young men were caught by them, and not being able to get free, there died a lamentable death.

Many a long year afterwards there came a king's son into that country, and heard an old man tell how there should be a castle standing behind the hedge of thorns, and that there a beautiful enchanted princess named Rosamond had slept for a hundred years, and with her the king and queen, and the whole court. The old man had been told by his grandfather that many king's sons had sought to pass the thorn-hedge, but had been caught and pierced by the thorns, and had died a miserable death. Then said the young man, "Nevertheless, I do not fear to try; I shall win through and see the lovely Rosamond." The good old man tried to dissuade him, but he would not listen to his words.

For now the hundred years were at an end, and the day had come when Rosamond should be awakened. When the prince drew near the hedge of thorns, it was changed into a hedge of beautiful large flowers, which parted and bent aside to let him pass, and then closed behind him in a thick hedge. When he reached the castle-yard, he saw the horses and brindled hunting-dogs lying asleep, and on the roof the pigeons were sitting with their heads under their wings. And when he came indoors, the flies on the wall were asleep, the cook in the kitchen had his hand uplifted to strike the scullion, and the kitchen-maid had the black fowl on her lap ready to pluck. Then he mounted higher, and saw in the hall the whole court lying asleep, and above them, on their thrones, slept the king and the queen. And still he went farther, and all was so quiet that he could hear his own breathing; and at last he came to the tower, and went up the winding stair, and opened the door of the little room where Rosamond lay. And when he saw her looking so lovely in her sleep, he could not turn away his eyes; and presently he stooped and kissed her, and she awaked, and opened her eyes, and looked very kindly on him. And she rose, and

She awaked, and opened her eyes, and looked very
kindly on him.

they went forth together, and the king and the queen and whole court waked up, and gazed on each other with great eyes of wonderment. And the horses in the yard got up and shook themselves, the hounds sprang up and wagged their tails, the pigeons on the roof drew their heads from under their wings, looked round, and flew into the field, the flies on the wall crept on a little farther, the kitchen fire leapt up and blazed, and cooked the meat, the joint on the spit began to roast, the cook gave the scullion such a box on the ear that he roared out, and the maid went on plucking the fowl.

Then the wedding of the prince and Rosamond was held with all splendour, and they lived very happily together until their lives' end.

The Golden Goose

THERE WAS a man who had three sons, the youngest of whom was called the Simpleton, and was despised, laughed at, and neglected, on every occasion. It happened one day that the eldest son wished to go into the forest to cut wood, and before he went his mother gave him a delicious pancake and a flask of wine, that he might not suffer from hunger or thirst. When he came into the forest a little old grey man met him, who wished him good day, and said,

"Give me a bit of cake out of your pocket, and let me have a drink of your wine; I am so hungry and thirsty."

But the prudent youth answered,

"Give you my cake and my wine? I haven't got any; be off with you."

And leaving the little man standing there, he went off. Then he began to fell a tree, but he had not been at it long before he made a wrong

8

stroke, and the hatchet hit him in the arm, so that he was obliged to go home and get it bound up. That was what came of the little grey man.

Afterwards the second son went into the wood, and the mother gave to him, as to the eldest, a pancake and a flask of wine. The little old grey man met him also, and begged for a little bit of cake and a drink of wine. But the second son spoke out plainly, saying,

"What I give you I lose myself, so be off with you."

And leaving the little man standing there, he went off. The punishment followed; as he was chopping away at the tree, he hit himself in the leg so severely that he had to be carried home.

Then said the Simpleton,

"Father, let me go for once into the forest to cut wood;" and the father answered, "Your brothers have hurt themselves by so doing; give it up, you understand nothing about it."

But the Simpleton went on begging so long, that the father said at last,

"Well, be off with you; you will only learn by experience."

The mother gave him a cake (it was only made with water, and baked in the ashes), and with it a flask of sour beer. When he came into the forest the little old grey man met him, and greeted him, saying,

"Give me a bit of your cake, and a drink from your flask; I am so hungry and thirsty."

And the Simpleton answered, "I have only a flour and water cake and sour beer; but if that is good enough for you, let us sit down together and eat." Then they sat down, and as the Simpleton took out his flour and water cake it became a rich pancake, and his sour beer became good wine; then they ate and drank, and afterwards the little man said,

"As you have such a kind heart, and share what you have so willingly, I will bestow good luck upon you. Yonder stands an old tree; cut it down, and at its roots you will find something," and thereupon the little man took his departure.

The Simpleton went there, and hewed away at the tree, and when it fell he saw, sitting among the roots, a goose with feathers of pure gold. He lifted it out and took it with him to an inn where he intended to stay the night. The landlord had three daughters who, when they saw the goose, were curious to know what wonderful kind of bird it was, and ended by longing for one of its golden feathers. The eldest thought, "I will wait for a good opportunity, and then I will pull out one of its feathers for myself;" and so, when the Simpleton was gone out, she seized the goose by its wing—but there her finger and hand had to stay, held fast. Soon after came the second sister

with the same idea of plucking out one of the
golden feathers for herself; but scarcely had she
touched her sister, than she also was obliged to
stay, held fast. Lastly came the third with the
same intentions; but the others screamed out,

"Stay away! for heaven's sake stay away!"

But she did not see why she should stay away,
and thought, "If they do so, why should not I?"
and went towards them. But when she reached
her sisters there she stopped, hanging on with
them. And so they had to stay, all night. The next
morning the Simpleton took the goose under his
arm and went away, unmindful of the three girls
that hung on to it. The three had always to run
after him, left and right, wherever his legs carried
him. In the midst of the fields they met the parson, who, when he saw the procession, said,

"Shame on you, girls, running after a young fellow through the fields like this," and forthwith he
seized hold of the youngest by the hand to drag
her away, but hardly had he touched her when he
too was obliged to run after them himself. Not
long after the sexton came that way, and seeing
the respected parson following at the heels of the
three girls, he called out,

"Ho, your reverence, whither away so quickly?
You forget that we have another christening to-
day;" and he seized hold of him by his gown; but
no sooner had he touched him than he was

obliged to follow on too. As the five tramped on, one after another, two peasants with their hoes came up from the fields, and the parson cried out to them, and begged them to come and set him and the sexton free, but no sooner had they touched the sexton than they had to follow on too; and now there were seven following the Simpleton and the goose.

By and by they came to a town where a king reigned, who had an only daughter who was so serious that no one could make her laugh; therefore the king had given out that whoever should make her laugh should have her in marriage. The Simpleton, when he heard this, went with his goose and his hangers-on into the presence of the king's daughter, and as soon as she saw the seven people following always one after the other, she burst out laughing, and seemed as if she could never stop. And so the Simpleton earned a right to her as his bride; but the king did not like him for a son-in-law and made all kinds of objections, and said he must first bring a man who could drink up a whole cellar of wine. The Simpleton thought that the little grey man would be able to help him, and went out into the forest, and there, on the very spot where he felled the tree, he saw a man sitting with a very sad countenance. The Simpleton asked him what was the matter, and he answered,

"I have a great thirst, which I cannot quench: cold water does not agree with me; I have indeed drunk up a whole cask of wine, but what good is a drop like that?"

Then said the Simpleton,

"I can help you; only come with me, and you shall have enough."

He took him straight to the king's cellar, and the man sat himself down before the big vats, and drank, and drank, and before a day was over he had drunk up the whole cellar-full. The Simpleton again asked for his bride, but the king was annoyed that a wretched fellow, called the Simpleton by everybody, should carry off his daughter, and so he made new conditions. He was to produce a man who could eat up a mountain of bread. The Simpleton did not hesitate long, but ran quickly off to the forest, and there in the same place sat a man who had fastened a strap round his body, making a very piteous face, and saying,

"I have eaten a whole bakehouse full of rolls, but what is the use of that when one is so hungry as I am? My stomach feels quite empty, and I am obliged to strap myself together, that I may not die of hunger."

The Simpleton was quite glad of this, and said,

"Get up quickly, and come along with me, and you shall have enough to eat."

He led him straight to the king's courtyard,

where all the meal in the kingdom had been collected and baked into a mountain of bread. The man out of the forest settled himself down before it and hastened to eat, and in one day the whole mountain had disappeared.

Then the Simpleton asked for his bride the third time. The king, however, found one more excuse, and said he must have a ship that should be able to sail on land or on water.

"So soon," said he, "as you come sailing along with it, you shall have my daughter for your wife."

The Simpleton went straight to the forest, and there sat the little old grey man with whom he had shared his cake, and he said,

"I have eaten for you, and I have drunk for you, I will also give you the ship; and all because you were kind to me at the first."

Then he gave him the ship that could sail on land and on water, and when the king saw it he knew he could no longer withhold his daughter. The marriage took place immediately, and at the death of the king the Simpleton possessed the kingdom, and lived long and happily with his wife.

Hansel and Gretel

NEAR A GREAT FOREST there lived a poor woodcutter and his wife, and his two children; the boy's name was Hansel and the girl's Gretel. They had very little to bite or to sup, and once, when there was great dearth in the land, the man could not even gain the daily bread. As he lay in bed one night thinking of this, and turning and tossing, he sighed heavily, and said to his wife,

"What will become of us? we cannot even feed our children; there is nothing left for ourselves."

"I will tell you what, husband," answered the wife; "we will take the children early in the morning into the forest, where it is thickest; we will make them a fire, and we will give each of them a piece of bread, then we will go to our work and leave them alone; they will never find the way home again, and we shall be quit of them."

"No, wife," said the man, "I cannot do that; I cannot find in my heart to take my children into the forest and to leave them there alone; the wild animals would soon come and devour them."

"O you fool," said she, "then we will all four starve; you had better get the coffins ready,"— and she left him no peace until he consented.

"But I really pity the poor children," said the man.

The two children had not been able to sleep for hunger, and had heard what their step-mother had said to their father. Gretel wept bitterly, and said to Hansel,

"It is all over with us."

"Do be quiet, Gretel," said Hansel, "and do not fret; I will manage something." And when the parents had gone to sleep he got up, put on his little coat, opened the back door, and slipped out. The moon was shining brightly, and the white flints that lay in front of the house glistened like pieces of silver. Hansel stooped and filled the little pocket of his coat as full as it would hold. Then he went back again, and said to Gretel,

"Be easy, dear little sister, and go to sleep quietly; God will not forsake us," and laid himself down again in his bed.

When the day was breaking, and before the sun had risen, the wife came and awakened the two children, saying,

"Get up, you lazy bones; we are going into the forest to cut wood."

Then she gave each of them a piece of bread, and said,

"That is for dinner, and you must not eat it before then, for you will get no more."

Gretel carried the bread under her apron, for Hansel had his pockets full of the flints. Then they set off all together on their way to the forest. When they had gone a little way Hansel stood still and looked back towards the house, and this he did again and again, till his father said to him,

"Hansel, what are you looking at? take care not to forget your legs."

"O father," said Hansel, "I am looking at my little white kitten, who is sitting up on the roof to bid me good-bye."

"You young fool," said the woman, "that is not your kitten, but the sunshine on the chimney-pot."

Of course Hansel had not been looking at his kitten, but had been taking every now and then a flint from his pocket and dropping it on the road.

When they reached the middle of the forest the father told the children to collect wood to make a fire to keep them warm; and Hansel and Gretel gathered brushwood enough for a little mountain; and it was set on fire, and when the flame was burning quite high the wife said,

"Now lie down by the fire and rest yourselves, you children, and we will go and cut wood; and when we are ready we will come and fetch you."

So Hansel and Gretel sat by the fire, and at noon they each ate their pieces of bread. They thought their father was in the wood all the time, as they seemed to hear the strokes of the axe: but really it was only a dry branch hanging to a withered tree that the wind moved to and fro. So when they had stayed there a long time their eyelids closed with weariness, and they fell fast asleep. When at last they woke it was night, and Gretel began to cry, and said,

"How shall we ever get out of this wood?" But Hansel comforted her, saying,

"Wait a little while longer, until the moon rises, and then we can easily find the way home."

And when the full moon got up Hansel took his little sister by the hand, and followed the way where the flint stones shone like silver, and showed them the road. They walked on the whole night through, and at the break of day they came to their father's house. They knocked at the door, and when the wife opened it and saw that it was Hansel and Gretel she said,

"You naughty children, why did you sleep so long in the wood? we thought you were never coming home again!"

But the father was glad, for it had gone to his heart to leave them both in the woods alone.

Not very long after that there was again great

scarcity in those parts, and the children heard their mother say at night in bed to their father,

"Everything is finished up; we have only half a loaf, and after that the tale comes to an end. The children must be off; we will take them farther into the wood this time, so that they shall not be able to find the way back again; there is no other way to manage."

The man felt sad at heart, and he thought,

"It would be better to share one's last morsel with one's children."

But the wife would listen to nothing that he said, but scolded and reproached him. He who says A must say B too, and when a man has given in once he has to do it a second time.

But the children were not asleep, and had heard all the talk. When the parents had gone to sleep Hansel got up to go out and get more flint stones, as he did before, but the wife had locked the door, and Hansel could not get out; but he comforted his little sister, and said,

"Don't cry, Gretel, and go to sleep quietly, and God will help us."

Early the next morning the wife came and pulled the children out of bed. She gave them each a little piece of bread—less than before; and on the way to the wood Hansel crumbled the bread in his pocket, and often stopped to throw a crumb on the ground.

"Hansel, what are you stopping behind and staring for?" said the father.

"I am looking at my little pigeon sitting on the roof, to say good-bye to me," answered Hansel.

"You fool," said the wife, "that is no pigeon, but the morning sun shining on the chimney-pot."

Hansel went on as before, and strewed bread crumbs all along the road.

The woman led the children far into the wood, where they had never been before in all their lives. And again there was a large fire made, and the mother said,

"Sit still there, you children, and when you are tired you can go to sleep; we are going into the forest to cut wood, and in the evening, when we are ready to go home, we will come and fetch you."

So when noon came Gretel shared her bread with Hansel, who had strewed his along the road. Then they went to sleep, and the evening passed, and no one came for the poor children. When they awoke it was dark night, and Hansel comforted his little sister, and said,

"Wait a little, Gretel, until the moon gets up, then we shall be able to see the way home by the crumbs of bread that I have scattered along it."

So when the moon rose they got up, but they could find no crumbs of bread, for the birds of the woods and of the fields had come and picked them up. Hansel thought they might find the way all the same, but they could not. They went on all that night, and the next day from the morning until the evening, but they could not find the way out of the wood, and they were very hungry, for they had nothing to eat but the few berries they could pick up. And when they were so tired that they could no longer drag themselves along, they lay down under a tree and fell asleep.

It was now the third morning since they had left their father's house. They were always trying to get back to it, but instead of that they only found themselves farther in the wood, and if help had not soon come they would have been starved. About noon they saw a pretty snow-white bird sitting on a bough, and singing so sweetly that they stopped to listen. And when he had finished the bird spread his wings and flew before them, and they followed after him until they came to a little house, and the bird perched on the roof, and when they came nearer they saw that the house was built of bread, and roofed with cakes; and the window was of transparent sugar.

"We will have some of this," said Hansel, "and make a fine meal. I will eat a piece of the roof, Gretel, and you can have some of the window—that will taste sweet."

So Hansel reached up and broke off a bit of the

roof, just to see how it tasted, and Gretel stood by the window and gnawed at it. Then they heard a thin voice call out from inside,

> "Nibble, nibble, like a mouse,
> Who is nibbling at my house?"

And the children answered,

> "Never mind,
> It is the wind."

And they went on eating, never disturbing themselves. Hansel, who found that the roof tasted very nice, took down a great piece of it, and Gretel pulled out a large round window-pane, and sat her down and began upon it. Then the door opened, and an aged woman came out, leaning upon a crutch. Hansel and Gretel felt very frightened, and let fall what they had in their hands. The old woman, however, nodded her head, and said,

"Ah, my dear children, how come you here? you must come indoors and stay with me, you will be no trouble."

So she took them each by the hand, and led them into her little house. And there they found a good meal laid out, of milk and pancakes, with sugar, apples, and nuts. After that she showed

"Ah, my dear children, how come you here?"

them two little white beds, and Hansel and Gretel laid themselves down on them, and thought they were in heaven.

The old woman, although her behaviour was so kind, was a wicked witch, who lay in wait for children, and had built the little house on purpose to entice them. When they were once inside she used to kill them, cook them, and eat them, and then it was a feast-day with her. The witch's eyes were red, and she could not see very far, but she had a keen scent, like the beasts, and knew very well when human creatures were near. When she knew that Hansel and Gretel were coming, she gave a spiteful laugh, and said triumphantly,

"I have them, and they shall not escape me!"

Early in the morning, before the children were awake, she got up to look at them, and as they lay sleeping so peacefully with round rosy cheeks, she said to herself,

"What a fine feast I shall have!"

Then she grasped Hansel with her withered hand, and led him into a little stable, and shut him up behind a grating; and call and scream as he might, it was no good. Then she went back to Gretel and shook her, crying,

"Get up, lazy bones; fetch water, and cook something nice for your brother; he is outside in the stable, and must be fattened up. And when he is fat enough I will eat him."

Gretel began to weep bitterly, but it was of no use, she had to do what the wicked witch bade her.

And so the best kind of victuals was cooked for poor Hansel, while Gretel got nothing but crab-shells. Each morning the old woman visited the little stable, and cried,

"Hansel, stretch out your finger, that I may tell if you will soon be fat enough."

Hansel, however, used to hold out a little bone, and the old woman, who had weak eyes, could not see what it was, and supposing it to be Hansel's finger, wondered very much that it was not getting fatter. When four weeks had passed and Hansel seemed to remain so thin, she lost patience and could wait no longer.

"Now then, Gretel," cried she to the little girl; "be quick and draw water; be Hansel fat or be he lean, to-morrow I must kill and cook him."

Oh what a grief for the poor little sister to have to fetch water, and how the tears flowed down over her cheeks!

"Dear God, pray help us!" cried she; "if we had been devoured by wild beasts in the wood at least we should have died together."

"Spare me your lamentations," said the old woman; "they are of no avail."

Early next morning Gretel had to get up, make the fire, and fill the kettle.

"First we will do the baking," said the old

woman; "I have heated the oven already, and kneaded the dough."

She pushed poor Gretel towards the oven, out of which the flames were already shining.

"Creep in," said the witch, "and see if it is properly hot, so that the bread may be baked."

And Gretel once in, she meant to shut the door upon her and let her be baked, and then she would have eaten her. But Gretel perceived her intention, and said,

"I don't know how to do it: how shall I get in?"

"Stupid goose," said the old woman, "the opening is big enough, do you see? I could get in myself!" and she stooped down and put her head in the oven's mouth. Then Gretel gave her a push, so that she went in farther, and she shut the iron door upon her, and put up the bar. Oh how frightfully she howled! but Gretel ran away, and left the wicked witch to burn miserably. Gretel went straight to Hansel, opened the stable-door, and cried,

"Hansel, we are free! the old witch is dead!"

Then out flew Hansel like a bird from its cage as soon as the door is opened. How rejoiced they both were! how they fell each on the other's neck! and danced about, and kissed each other! And as they had nothing more to fear they went over all the old witch's house, and in every corner there stood chests of pearls and precious stones.

"This is something better than flint stones," said Hansel, as he filled his pockets, and Gretel, thinking she also would like to carry something home with her, filled her apron full.

"Now, away we go," said Hansel;—"if we only can get out of the witch's wood."

When they had journeyed a few hours they came to a great piece of water.

"We can never get across this," said Hansel, "I see no stepping-stones and no bridge."

"And there is no boat either," said Gretel; "but here comes a white duck; if I ask her she will help us over." So she cried,

> "Duck, duck, here we stand,
>   Hansel and Gretel, on the land,
>   Stepping-stones and bridge we lack,
>   Carry us over on your nice white back."

And the duck came accordingly, and Hansel got upon her and told his sister to come too.

"No," answered Gretel, "that would be too hard upon the duck; we can go separately, one after the other."

And that was how it was managed, and after that they went on happily, until they came to the wood, and the way grew more and more familiar, till at last they saw in the distance their father's house. Then they ran till they came up to it, rushed in at the door, and fell on their father's neck. The man had not had a quiet hour since he left his children in the wood; but the wife was dead. And when Gretel opened her apron the pearls and precious stones were scattered all over the room, and Hansel took one handful after another out of his pocket. Then was all care at an end, and they lived in great joy together.

The Bremen Town Musicians

THERE WAS ONCE an ass whose master had made him carry sacks to the mill for many a long year, but whose strength began at last to fail, so that each day as it came found him less capable of work. Then his master began to think of turning him out, but the ass, guessing that something was in the wind that boded him no good, ran away, taking the road to Bremen; for there he thought he might get an engagement as town musician. When he had gone a little way he found a hound lying by the side of the road panting, as if he had run a long way.

"Now, Holdfast, what are you so out of breath about?" said the ass.

"Oh dear!" said the dog, "now I am old, I get weaker every day, and can do no good in the hunt, so, as my master was going to have me killed, I have made my escape; but now, how am I to gain a living?"

"I will tell you what," said the ass, "I am going

to Bremen to become town musician. You may as well go with me, and take up music too. I can play the lute, and you can beat the drum."

And the dog consented, and they walked on together. It was not long before they came to a cat sitting in the road, looking as dismal as three wet days.

"Now then, what is the matter with you, old shaver?" said the ass.

"I should like to know who would be cheerful when his neck is in danger," answered the cat. "Now that I am old my teeth are getting blunt, and I would rather sit by the oven and purr than run about after mice, and my mistress wanted to drown me; so I took myself off; but good advice is scarce, and I do not know what is to become of me."

"Go with us to Bremen," said the ass, "and become town musician. You understand serenading."

The cat thought well of the idea, and went with them accordingly. After that the three travellers passed by a yard, and a cock was perched on the gate crowing with all his might.

"Your cries are enough to pierce bone and marrow," said the ass; "what is the matter?"

"I have foretold good weather for Lady-day, so that all the shirts may be washed and dried; and now on Sunday morning company is coming, and the mistress has told the cook that I must be made into soup, and this evening my neck is to be wrung, so that I am crowing with all my might while I can."

"You had much better go with us, Chanticleer," said the ass. "We are going to Bremen. At any rate that will be better than dying. You have a powerful voice, and when we are all performing together it will have a very good effect."

So the cock consented, and they went on all four together.

But Bremen was too far off to be reached in one day, and towards evening they came to a wood, where they determined to pass the night. The ass and the dog lay down under a large tree; the cat got up among the branches, and the cock flew up to the top, as that was the safest place for him. Before he went to sleep he looked all round him to the four points of the compass, and perceived in the distance a little light shining, and he called out to his companions that there must be a house not far off, as he could see a light, so the ass said,

"We had better get up and go there, for these are uncomfortable quarters." The dog began to fancy a few bones, not quite bare, would do him good. And they all set off in the direction of the light, and it grew larger and brighter, until at last it led them to a robber's house, all lighted up. The ass, being the biggest, went up to the window, and looked in.

"Well, what do you see?" asked the dog.

"What do I see?" answered the ass; "here is a table set out with splendid eatables and drinkables, and robbers sitting at it and making themselves very comfortable."

"That would just suit us," said the cock.

"Yes, indeed, I wish we were there," said the ass. Then they consulted together how it should be managed so as to get the robbers out of the house, and at last they hit on a plan. The ass was to place his forefeet on the window-sill, the dog was to get on the ass's back, the cat on the top of the dog, and lastly the cock was to fly up and perch on the cat's head. When that was done, at a given signal they all began to perform their music. The ass brayed, the dog barked, the cat mewed, and the cock crowed; then they burst through into the room, breaking all the panes of glass. The robbers fled at the dreadful sound; they thought it was some goblin, and fled to the wood in the utmost terror. Then the four companions sat down to table, made free with the remains of the meal, and feasted as if they had been hungry for a month. And when they had finished they put out the lights, and each sought out a sleeping-place to suit his nature and habits. The ass laid himself down outside on the dunghill, the dog behind the door, the cat on the hearth by the warm ashes, and the cock settled himself in the cockloft, and as they were all tired with their long journey they soon fell fast asleep.

When midnight drew near, and the robbers from afar saw that no light was burning, and that everything appeared quiet, their captain said to them that he thought that they had run away without reason, telling one of them to go and reconnoitre. So one of them went, and found everything quite quiet; he went into the kitchen to strike a light, and taking the glowing fiery eyes of the cat for burning coals, he held a match to them in order to kindle it. But the cat, not seeing the joke, flew into his face, spitting and scratching. Then he cried out in terror, and ran to get out at the back door, but the dog, who was lying there, ran at him and bit his leg; and as he was rushing through the yard by the dunghill the ass struck out and gave him a great kick with his hindfoot; and the cock, who had been wakened with the noise, and felt quite brisk, cried out, "Cock-a-doodle-doo!"

Then the robber got back as well as he could to his captain, and said, "Oh dear! in that house there is a grewsome witch, and I felt her breath and her long nails in my face; and by the door there stands a man who stabbed me in the leg with a knife; and in the yard there lies a black spectre, who beat me with his wooden club; and above, upon the roof, there sits the justice, who cried, 'Bring that rogue here!' And so I ran away from the place as fast as I could."

From that time forward the robbers never ventured to that house, and the four Bremen town musicians found themselves so well off where they were, that there they stayed. And the person who last related this tale is still living, as you see.

The Golden Bird

IN TIMES gone by there was a king who had at the back of his castle a beautiful pleasure-garden, in which stood a tree that bore golden apples. As the apples ripened they were counted, but one morning one was missing. Then the king was angry, and he ordered that watch should be kept about the tree every night. Now the king had three sons, and he sent the eldest to spend the whole night in the garden; so he watched till midnight, and then he could keep off sleep no longer, and in the morning another apple was missing. The second son had to watch the following night; but it fared no better, for when twelve o'clock had struck he went to sleep, and in the morning another apple was missing. Now came the turn of the third son to watch, and he was ready to do so; but the king had less trust in him, and believed he would acquit himself still worse than his brothers, but in the end he consented to let him try. So the young man lay down under the tree to watch, and resolved that sleep should not be master. When it struck twelve something came rushing through the air, and he saw in the moonlight a bird flying towards him, whose feathers glittered like gold. The bird perched upon the tree, and had already pecked off an apple, when the young man let fly an arrow at it. The bird flew away, but the arrow had struck its plumage, and one of its golden feathers fell to the ground; the young man picked it up, and taking it next morning to the king, told him what had happened in the night. The king called his council together, and all declared that such a feather was worth more than the whole kingdom.

"Since the feather is so valuable," said the king, "one is not enough for me; I must and will have the whole bird."

So the eldest son set off, and relying on his own cleverness he thought he should soon find the golden bird. When he had gone some distance he saw a fox sitting at the edge of a wood, and he pointed his gun at him. The fox cried out,

"Do not shoot me, and I will give you good counsel. You are on your way to find the golden bird, and this evening you will come to a village, in which two taverns stand facing each other. One will be brightly lighted up, and there will be plenty of merriment going on inside; do not mind about that, but go into the other one, although it will look to you very uninviting."

"How can a silly beast give one any rational advice?" thought the king's son, and let fly at the fox, but missed him, and he stretched out his tail and ran quick into the wood. Then the young man went on his way, and towards evening he came to the village, and there stood the two taverns; in one singing and dancing was going on, the other looked quite dull and wretched. "I should be a fool," said he, "to go into that dismal place, while there is anything so good close by." So he went into the merry inn, and there lived in clover, quite forgetting the bird and his father, and all good counsel.

As time went on, and the eldest son never came home, the second son set out to seek the golden bird. He met with the fox, just as the eldest did, and received good advice from him without attending to it. And when he came to the two taverns, his brother was standing and calling to him at the window of one of them, out of which came sounds of merriment; so he could not resist, but went in and revelled to his heart's content.

And then, as time went on, the youngest son wished to go forth, and to try his luck, but his father would not consent.

"It would be useless," said he; "he is much less likely to find the bird than his brothers, and if any misfortune were to happen to him he would not know how to help himself; his wits are none of the best."

But at last, as there was no peace to be had, he let him go. By the side of the wood sat the fox, begged him to spare his life, and gave him good counsel. The young man was kind, and said,

"Be easy, little fox, I will do you no harm."

"You shall not repent of it," answered the fox, "and that you may get there all the sooner, get up and sit on my tail."

And no sooner had he done so than the fox began to run, and off they went over stock and stone, so that the wind whistled in their hair. When they reached the village the young man got down, and, following the fox's advice, went into the mean-looking tavern, without hesitating, and there he passed a quiet night. The next morning, when he went out into the field, the fox, who was sitting there already, said,

"I will tell you further what you have to do. Go straight on until you come to a castle, before which a great band of soldiers lie, but do not trouble yourself about them, for they will be all asleep and snoring; pass through them and forward into the castle, and go through all the rooms, until you come to one where there is a golden bird hanging in a wooden cage. Near at hand will stand empty a golden cage of state, but you must beware of taking the bird out of his ugly cage and putting him into the fine one; if you do so you will come to harm."

After he had finished saying this the fox stretched out his tail again, and the king's son sat him down upon it; then away they went over stock and stone, so that the wind whistled through their hair. And when the king's son reached the castle he found everything as the fox had said: and he at last entered the room where the golden bird was hanging in a wooden cage, while a golden one was standing by; the three golden apples too were in the room. Then, thinking it foolish to let the beautiful bird stay in that mean and ugly cage, he opened the door of it, took hold of it, and put it in

the golden one. In the same moment the
bird uttered a piercing cry. The soldiers
awaked, rushed in, seized the king's son and
put him in prison. The next morning he was
brought before a judge, and, as he confessed
everything, condemned to death. But the king
said he would spare his life on one condition,
that he should bring him the golden horse
whose paces were swifter than the wind, and
that then he should also receive the golden
bird as a reward.

So the king's son set off to find the golden
horse, but he sighed, and was very sad, for how
should it be accomplished? And then he saw
his old friend the fox sitting by the roadside.

"Now, you see," said the fox, "all this has
happened, because you would not listen to me.
But be of good courage, I will bring you
through, and will tell you how you are to get
the golden horse. You must go straight on until
you come to a castle, where the horse stands in
his stable; before the stable-door the grooms
will be lying, but they will all be asleep and
snoring; and you can go and quietly lead out
the horse. But one thing you must mind—take
care to put upon him the plain saddle of wood
and leather, and not the golden one, which will

hang close by; otherwise it will go badly with you."

Then the fox stretched out his tail, and the king's son seated himself upon it, and away they went over stock and stone until the wind whistled through their hair. And everything happened just as the fox had said, and he came to the stall where the golden horse was: and as he was about to put on him the plain saddle, he thought to himself,

"Such a beautiful animal would be disgraced were I not to put on him the good saddle, which becomes him so well." However, no sooner did the horse feel the golden saddle touch him than he began to neigh. And the grooms all awoke, seized the king's son and threw him into prison. The next morning he was delivered up to justice and condemned to death, but the king promised him his life, and also to bestow upon him the golden horse, if he could convey thither the beautiful princess of the golden castle.

With a heavy heart the king's son set out, but by great good luck he soon met with the faithful fox.

"I ought now to leave you to your own ill-luck," said the fox, "but I am sorry for you, and will once more help you in your need. Your way lies straight up to the golden castle: you will arrive there in the evening, and at night, when all is quiet, the beautiful princess goes to the bath. And as she is entering the bathing-house, go up to her and give her a kiss, then she will follow you, and you can lead her away; but do not suffer her first to go and take leave of her parents, or it will go ill with you."

Then the fox stretched out his tail; the king's son seated himself upon it, and away they went over stock and stone, so that the wind whistled through their hair. And when he came to the golden castle all was as the fox had said. He waited until midnight, when all lay in deep sleep, and then as the beautiful princess went to the bathing-house he went up to her and gave her a kiss, and she willingly promised to go with him, but she begged him earnestly, and with tears, that he would let her first go and take leave of her parents. At first he denied her prayer, but as she wept so much the more, and fell at his feet, he gave in at last. And no sooner had the princess reached her father's bedside than he, and all who were in the castle, waked up, and the young man was seized and thrown into prison.

The next morning the king said to him,

"Thy life is forfeit, but thou shalt find grace if thou canst level that mountain that lies before my windows, and over which I am not able to see: and if this is done within eight days thou shalt have my daughter for a reward."

So the king's son set to work, and dug and shovelled away without ceasing, but when, on the seventh day, he saw how little he had accomplished, and that all his work was as nothing, he fell into great sadness, and gave up all hope. But on the evening of the seventh day the fox appeared, and said,

"You do not deserve that I should help you, but go now and lie down to sleep, and I will do the work for you."

The next morning when he awoke, and looked out of the window, the mountain had disappeared. The young man hastened full of joy to the king, and told him that his behest was fulfilled, and, whether the king liked it or not, he had to keep to his word, and let his daughter go.

So they both went away together, and it was not long before the faithful fox came up to them.

"Well, you have got the best first," said he; "but you must know the golden horse

The king's son carried off the beautiful princess
on the golden horse.

belongs to the princess of the golden castle."

"But how shall I get it?" asked the young man.

"I am going to tell you," answered the fox. "First, go to the king who sent you to the golden castle, and take to him the beautiful princess. There will then be very great rejoicing; he will willingly give you the golden horse, and they will lead him out to you; then mount him without delay, and stretch out your hand to each of them to take leave, and last of all to the princess, and when you have her by the hand swing her up on the horse behind you, and off you go! Nobody will be able to overtake you, for that horse goes swifter than the wind."

And so it was all happily done, and the king's son carried off the beautiful princess on the golden horse. The fox did not stay behind, and he said to the young man,

"Now, I will help you to get the golden bird. When you draw near the castle where the bird is, let the lady alight, and I will take her under my care; then you must ride the golden horse into the castle-yard, and there will be great rejoicing to see it, and they will bring out to you the golden bird; as soon as you have the cage in your hand, you must start off back to us, and then you shall carry the lady away."

The plan was successfully carried out; and when the young man returned with the treasure, the fox said,

"Now, what will you give me for my reward?"

"What would you like?" asked the young man.

"When we are passing through the wood, I desire that you should slay me, and cut my head and feet off."

"That were a strange sign of gratitude," said the king's son, "and I could not possibly do such a thing."

Then said the fox,

"If you will not do it, I must leave you; but before I go let me give you some good advice. Beware of two things: buy no gallows-meat, and sit at no brook-side." With that the fox ran off into the wood.

The young man thought to himself, "That is a wonderful animal, with most singular ideas. How should any one buy gallows-meat? and I am sure I have no particular fancy for sitting by a brook-side."

So he rode on with the beautiful princess, and their way led them through the village where his two brothers had stayed. There they heard great outcry and noise, and when he asked what it was all about, they told him that two people were going to be hanged. And when he drew near he saw that it was his two brothers, who had done all sorts of evil tricks, and had wasted all their goods. He asked if there were no means of setting them free.

"Oh yes! if you will buy them off," answered the people; "but why should you spend your money in redeeming such worthless men?"

But he persisted in doing so; and when they were let go they all went on their journey together.

After a while they came to the wood where the fox had met them first, and there it seemed so cool and sheltered from the sun's burning rays that the two brothers said,

"Let us rest here for a little by the brook, and eat and drink to refresh ourselves."

The young man consented, quite forgetting the fox's warning, and he seated himself by the brook-side, suspecting no evil. But the two brothers thrust him backwards into the brook, seized the princess, the horse, and the bird, and went home to their father.

"Is not this the golden bird that we bring?" said they; "and we have also the golden horse, and the princess of the golden castle."

Then there was great rejoicing in the royal castle, but the horse did not feed, the bird did not chirp, and the princess sat still and wept.

The youngest brother, however, had not perished. The brook was, by good fortune, dry, and he fell on soft moss without receiving any hurt, but he could not get up again. But in his need the faithful fox was not lacking; he came up running, and reproached him for having forgotten his advice.

"But I cannot forsake you all the same," said he; "I will help you back again into daylight." So he told the young man to grasp his tail, and hold on to it fast, and so he drew him up again.

"Still you are not quite out of all danger," said the fox; "your brothers, not being certain of your death, have surrounded the wood with sentinels, who are to put you to death if you let yourself be seen."

A poor beggar-man was sitting by the path, and the young man changed clothes with him, and went clad in that wise into the king's courtyard. Nobody knew him, but the bird began to chirp, and the horse began to feed, and the beautiful princess ceased weeping.

"What does this mean?" said the king, astonished.

The princess answered,

"I cannot tell, except that I was sad, and now I am joyful; it is to me as if my rightful bridegroom had returned."

Then she told him all that happened, although the two brothers had threatened to put her to death if she let out anything. The king then ordered every person who was in the castle to be brought before him, and with the rest came the young man like a beggar in his wretched garments; but the princess knew him, and greeted him well, falling on his neck and kissing him. The wicked brothers were seized and put to death, and the youngest brother was married to the princess, and succeeded to the inheritance of his father.

But what became of the poor fox? Long afterwards the king's son was going through the wood, and the fox met him and said,

"Now, you have everything that you can wish for, but my misfortunes never come to an end, and it lies in your power to free me from them." And once more he prayed the king's son earnestly to slay him, and cut off his head and feet. So, at last, he consented, and no sooner was it done than the fox was changed into a man, and was no other than the brother of the beautiful princess; and thus he was set free from a spell that had bound him for a long, long time.

And now, indeed, there lacked nothing to their happiness as long as they lived.

The Frog Prince

IN THE OLD TIMES, when it was still of some use to wish for the thing one wanted, there lived a King whose daughters were all handsome, but the youngest was so beautiful that the sun himself, who has seen so much, wondered each time he shone over her because of her beauty. Near the royal castle there was a great dark wood, and in the wood under an old linden-tree was a well; and when the day was hot, the King's daughter used to go forth into the wood and sit by the brink of the cool well, and if the time seemed long, she would take out a golden ball, and throw it up and catch it again, and this was her favourite pastime.

Now it happened one day that the golden ball, instead of falling back into the maiden's little hand which had sent it aloft, dropped to the ground near the edge of the well and rolled in. The King's daughter followed it with her eyes as it sank, but the well was deep, so deep that the bottom could not be seen. Then she began to weep, and she wept and wept as if she could never be comforted. And in the midst of her weeping she heard a voice saying to her,

"What ails thee, King's daughter? thy tears would melt a heart of stone."

And when she looked to see where the voice came from, there was nothing but a frog stretching his thick ugly head out of the water.

"Oh, is it you, old waddler?" said she; "I weep because my golden ball has fallen into the well."

"Never mind, do not weep," answered the frog; "I can help you; but what will you give me if I fetch up your ball again?"

"Whatever you like, dear frog," said she; "any of my clothes, my pearls and jewels, or even the golden crown that I wear."

"Thy clothes, thy pearls and jewels, and thy golden crown are not for me," answered the frog; "but if thou wouldst love me, and have me for thy companion and play-fellow, and let me sit by thee at table, and eat from thy plate, and drink from thy cup, and sleep in thy little bed,—if thou wouldst promise all this, then would I dive below the water and fetch thee thy golden ball again."

"Oh yes," she answered; "I will promise it all, whatever you want, if you will only get me my ball again."

But she thought to herself, "What nonsense he

talks! as if he could do anything but sit in the water and croak with the other frogs, or could possibly be any one's companion."

But the frog, as soon as he heard her promise, drew his head under the water and sank down out of sight, but after a while he came to the surface again with the ball in his mouth, and he threw it on the grass.

The King's daughter was overjoyed to see her pretty plaything again, and she caught it up and ran off with it.

"Stop, stop!" cried the frog; "take me up too; I cannot run as fast as you!"

But it was of no use, for croak, croak after her as he might, she would not listen to him, but made haste home, and very soon forgot all about the poor frog, who had to betake himself to his well again.

The next day, when the King's daughter was sitting at table with the King and all the court, and eating from her golden plate, there came something pitter patter up the marble stairs, and then there came a knocking at the door, and a voice crying "Youngest King's daughter, let me in!"

And she got up and ran to see who it could be, but when she opened the door, there was the frog sitting outside. Then she shut the door hastily and went back to her seat, feeling very uneasy.

The King noticed how quickly her heart was beating, and said,

"My child, what are you afraid of? is there a giant standing at the door ready to carry you away?"

"Oh no," answered she; "no giant, but a horrid frog."

"And what does the frog want?" asked the King.

"O dear father," answered she, "when I was sitting by the well yesterday, and playing with my golden ball, it fell into the water, and while I was crying for the loss of it, the frog came and got it again for me on condition I would let him be my companion, but I never thought that he could leave the water and come after me; but now there he is outside the door, and he wants to come in to me."

And then they all heard him knocking the second time and crying,

> "Youngest King's daughter,
> Open to me!
> By the well water
> What promised you me?
> Youngest King's daughter,
> Now open to me!"

"That which thou hast promised must thou perform," said the King; "so go now and let him in."

So she went and opened the door, and the frog hopped in, following at her heels, till she reached her chair. Then he stopped and cried,

"Lift me up to sit by you."

But she delayed doing so until the King ordered her. When once the frog was on the chair, he wanted to get on the table, and there he sat and said,

"Now push your golden plate a little nearer, so that we may eat together."

And so she did, but everybody might see how unwilling she was, and the frog feasted heartily, but every morsel seemed to stick in her throat.

"I have had enough now," said the frog at last, "and as I am tired, you must carry me to your room, and make ready your silken bed, and we will lie down and go to sleep."

Then the King's daughter began to weep, and was afraid of the cold frog, that nothing would satisfy him but he must sleep in her pretty clean bed. Now the King grew angry with her, saying,

"That which thou hast promised in thy time of necessity, must thou now perform."

So she picked up the frog with her finger and thumb, carried him upstairs and put him in a corner, and when she had lain down to sleep, he came creeping up, saying, "I am tired and want sleep as much as you; take me up, or I will tell your father."

Then she felt beside herself with rage, and

picking him up, she threw him with all her strength against the wall, crying,

"Now will you be quiet, you horrid frog!"

But as he fell, he ceased to be a frog, and became all at once a prince with beautiful kind eyes. And it came to pass that, with her father's consent, they became bride and bridegroom. And he told her how a wicked witch had bound him by her spells, and how no one but she alone could have released him, and that they two would go together to his father's kingdom. And there came to the door a carriage drawn by eight white horses, with white plumes on their heads, and with golden harness, and behind the carriage was standing faithful Henry, the servant of the young prince. Now, faithful Henry had suffered such care and pain when his master was turned into a frog, that he had been obliged to wear three iron bands over his heart, to keep it from breaking with trouble and anxiety. When the carriage started to take the prince to his kingdom, and faithful Henry had helped them both in, he got up behind, and was full of joy at his master's deliverance. And when they had gone a part of the way, the prince heard a sound at the back of the carriage, as if something had broken, and he turned round and cried,

"Henry, the wheel must be breaking!" but Henry answered,

"The wheel does not break,
'Tis the band round my heart
That, to lessen its ache,
When I grieved for your sake,
I bound round my heart."

Again, and yet once again there was the same sound, and the prince thought it must be the wheel breaking, but it was the breaking of the other bands from faithful Henry's heart, because it was now so relieved and happy.

Rumpelstiltskin

THERE WAS ONCE a miller who was poor, but he had one beautiful daughter. It happened one day that he came to speak with the king, and, to give himself consequence, he told him that he had a daughter who could spin gold out of straw. The king said to the miller,

"That is an art that pleases me well; if thy daughter is as clever as you say, bring her to my castle to-morrow, that I may put her to the proof."

When the girl was brought to him, he led her into a room that was quite full of straw, and gave her a wheel and spindle, and said,

"Now set to work, and if by the early morning thou hast not spun this straw to gold thou shalt die." And he shut the door himself, and left her there alone.

And so the poor miller's daughter was left there sitting, and could not think what to do for her life: she had no notion how to set to work to spin gold from straw, and her distress grew so great that she began to weep. Then all at once the door opened, and in came a little man, who said,

"Good evening, miller's daughter; why are you crying?"

"Oh!" answered the girl, "I have got to spin gold out of straw, and I don't understand the business."

Then the little man said,

"What will you give me if I spin it for you?"

"My necklace," said the girl.

The little man took the necklace, seated himself before the wheel, and whirr, whirr, whirr! three times round and the bobbin was full; then he took up another, and whirr, whirr, whirr! three times round, and that was full; and so he went on till the morning, when all the straw had been spun, and all the bobbins were full of gold. At sunrise came the king, and when he saw the gold he was astonished and very much rejoiced, for he was very avaricious. He had the miller's daughter taken into another room filled with straw, much bigger than the last, and told her that as she valued her life she must spin it all in one night. The girl did not know what to do, so she began to cry, and then the door opened, and the little man appeared and said,

"What will you give me if I spin all this straw into gold?"

"The ring from my finger," answered the girl.

So the little man took the ring, and began again to send the wheel whirring round, and by the next morning all the straw was spun into glistening gold. The king was rejoiced beyond measure at the sight, but as he could never have enough of gold, he had the miller's daughter taken into a still larger room full of straw, and said,

"This, too, must be spun in one night, and if you accomplish it you shall be my wife." For he thought, "Although she is but a miller's daughter, I am not likely to find any one richer in the whole world."

As soon as the girl was left alone, the little man appeared for the third time and said,

"What will you give me if I spin the straw for you this time?"

"I have nothing left to give," answered the girl.

"Then you must promise me the first child you have after you are queen," said the little man.

"But who knows whether that will happen?" thought the girl; but as she did not know what else to do in her necessity, she promised the little man what he desired, upon which he began to spin, until all the straw was gold. And when in the morning the king came and found all done according to his wish, he caused the wedding to be held at once, and the miller's pretty daughter became a queen.

In a year's time she brought a fine child into the world, and thought no more of the little man;

but one day he came suddenly into her room, and said,

"Now give me what you promised me."

The queen was terrified greatly, and offered the little man all the riches of the kingdom if he would only leave the child; but the little man said,

"No, I would rather have something living than all the treasures of the world."

Then the queen began to lament and to weep, so that the little man had pity upon her.

"I will give you three days," said he, "and if at the end of that time you cannot tell my name, you must give up the child to me."

Then the queen spent the whole night in thinking over all the names that she had ever heard, and sent a messenger through the land to ask far and wide for all the names that could be found. And when the little man came next day, (beginning with Caspar, Melchior, Balthazar) she repeated all she knew, and went through the whole list, but after each the little man said,

"That is not my name."

The second day the queen sent to inquire of all the neighbours what the servants were called, and told the little man all the most unusual and singular names, saying,

"Perhaps you are called Roast-ribs, or Sheepshanks, or Spindleshanks?" But he answered nothing but,

"That is not my name."

"The devil told you that! the devil told you that!" cried
the little man.

The third day the messenger came back again, and said,

"I have not been able to find one single new name; but as I passed through the woods I came to a high hill, and near it was a little house, and before the house burned a fire, and round the fire danced a comical little man, and he hopped on one leg and cried,

"To-day do I bake, to-morrow I brew,
    The day after that the queen's child comes in;
And oh! I am glad that nobody knew
    That the name I am called is Rumpelstiltskin!"

You cannot think how pleased the queen was to hear that name, and soon afterwards, when the little man walked in and said, "Now, Mrs. Queen, what is my name?" she said at first,

"Are you called Jack?"

"No," answered he.

"Are you called Harry?" she asked again.

"No," answered he. And then she said,

"Then perhaps your name is Rumpelstiltskin!"

"The devil told you that! the devil told you that!" cried the little man, and in his anger he stamped with his right foot so hard that it went into the ground above his knee; then he seized his left foot with both his hands in such a fury that he split in two, and there was an end of him.

Little Red Riding Hood

THERE WAS ONCE a sweet little maid, much beloved by everybody, but most of all by her grandmother, who never knew how to make enough of her. Once she sent her a little cloak of red velvet, and as it was very becoming to her, and she never wore anything else, people called her Little Red Riding Hood. One day her mother said to her,

"Come, Little Red Riding Hood, here are some cakes and a flask of wine for you to take to grandmother; she is weak and ill, and they will do her good. Make haste and start before it grows hot, and walk properly and nicely, and don't run, or you might fall and break the flask of wine, and there would be none left for grandmother. And when you go into her room, don't forget to say, Good morning, instead of staring about you."

"I will be sure to take care," said Little Red Riding Hood to her mother, and gave her hand upon it. Now the grandmother lived away in the wood, half-an-hour's walk from the village; and when Little Red Riding Hood had reached the wood, she met the wolf; but as she did not know what a bad sort of animal he was, she did not feel frightened.

"Good day, Little Red Riding Hood," said he.

"Thank you kindly, Wolf," answered she.

"Where are you going so early, Little Red Riding Hood?"

"To my grandmother's."

"What are you carrying under your apron?"

"Cakes and wine; we baked yesterday; and my grandmother is very weak and ill, so they will do her good, and strengthen her."

"Where does your grandmother live, Little Red Riding Hood?"

"A quarter of an hour's walk from here; her house stands beneath the three oak trees, and you may know it by the hazel bushes," said Little Red Riding Hood. The wolf thought to himself,

"That tender young thing would be a delicious morsel, and would taste better than the old one; I must manage somehow to get both of them."

Then he walked by Little Red Riding Hood a little while, and said,

"Little Red Riding Hood, just look at the pretty flowers that are growing all round you, and I don't think you are listening to the song of the birds; you are posting along just as if you were going to school, and it is so delightful out here in the wood."

Little Red Riding Hood glanced round her, and when she saw the sunbeams darting here and there through the trees, and lovely flowers everywhere, she thought to herself,

"If I were to take a fresh nosegay to my grandmother she would be very pleased, and it is so early in the day that I shall reach her in plenty of time;" and so she ran about in the wood, looking for flowers. And as she picked one she saw a still prettier one a little farther off, and so she went farther and farther into the wood. But the wolf went straight to the grandmother's house and knocked at the door.

"Who is there?" cried the grandmother.

"Little Red Riding Hood," he answered, "and I have brought you some cake and wine. Please open the door."

"Lift the latch," cried the grandmother; "I am too feeble to get up."

So the wolf lifted the latch, and the door flew open, and he fell on the grandmother and ate her up without saying one word. Then he drew on her clothes, put on her cap, lay down in her bed, and drew the curtains.

Little Red Riding Hood was all this time running about among the flowers, and when she had gathered as many as she could hold, she remembered her grandmother, and set off to go to her. She was surprised to find the door standing open, and when she came in side she felt very strange, and thought to herself,

"Oh dear, how uncomfortable I feel, and I was so glad this morning to go to my grandmother!"

And when she said, "Good morning," there was no answer. Then she went up to the bed and drew back the curtains; there lay the grandmother with her cap pulled over her eyes, so that she looked very odd.

"O grandmother, what large ears you have got!"

"The better to hear with."

"O grandmother, what great eyes you have got!"

"The better to see with."

"O grandmother, what large hands you have got!"

"The better to take hold of you with."

"But, grandmother, what a terrible large mouth you have got!"

"The better to devour you!" And no sooner had the wolf said it than he made one bound from the bed, and swallowed up poor Little Red Riding Hood.

Then the wolf, having satisfied his hunger, lay

"O grandmother, what large ears you have got!"

down again in the bed, went to sleep, and began to snore loudly. The huntsman heard him as he was passing by the house, and thought,

"How the old woman snores—I had better see if there is anything the matter with her."

Then he went into the room, and walked up to the bed, and saw the wolf lying there.

"At last I find you, you old sinner!" said he; "I have been looking for you a long time." And he made up his mind that the wolf had swallowed the grandmother whole, and that she might yet be saved. So he did not fire, but took a pair of shears and began to slit up the wolf's body. When he made a few snips Little Red Riding Hood appeared, and after a few more snips she jumped out and cried, "Oh dear, how frightened I have been! it is so dark inside the wolf." And then out came the old grandmother, still living and breathing. But Little Red Riding Hood went and quickly fetched some large stones, with which she filled the wolf's body, so that when he waked up, and was going to rush away, the stones were so heavy that he sank down and fell dead.

They were all three very pleased. The huntsman took off the wolf's skin, and carried it home. The grandmother ate the cakes, and drank the wine, and held up her head again, and Little Red Riding Hood said to herself that she would never more stray about in the wood alone, but would mind what her mother told her.

It must also be related how a few days afterwards, when Little Red Riding Hood was again taking cakes to her grandmother, another wolf spoke to her, and wanted to tempt her to leave the path; but she was on her guard, and went straight on her way, and told her grandmother how that the wolf had met her, and wished her good-day, but had looked so wicked about the eyes that she thought if it had not been on the high road he would have devoured her.

"Come," said the grandmother, "we will shut the door, so that he may not get in."

Soon after came the wolf knocking at the door, and calling out, "Open the door, grandmother, I am Little Red Riding Hood, bringing you cakes." But they remained still, and did not open the door. After that the wolf slunk by the house, and got at last upon the roof to wait until Little Red Riding Hood should return home in the evening; then he meant to spring down upon her, and devour her in the darkness. But the grandmother discovered his plot. Now there stood before the house a great stone trough, and the grandmother said to the child, "Little Red Riding Hood, I was boiling sausages yesterday, so take the bucket, and carry away the water they were boiled in, and pour it into the trough."

And Little Red Riding Hood did so until the great trough was quite full. When the smell of the sausages reached the nose of the wolf he snuffed it up, and looked round, and stretched out his neck so far that he lost his balance and began to slip, and he slipped down off the roof straight into the great trough, and was drowned. Then Little Red Riding Hood went cheerfully home, and came to no harm.

Tom Thumb

THERE WAS ONCE a poor countryman who used to sit in the chimney-corner all evening and poke the fire, while his wife sat at her spinning-wheel.

And he used to say,

"How dull it is without any children about us; our house is so quiet, and other people's houses so noisy and merry!"

"Yes," answered his wife, and sighed, "if we could only have one, and that one ever so little, no bigger than my thumb, how happy I should be! It would, indeed, be having our heart's desire."

Now, it happened that after a while the woman had a child who was perfect in all his limbs, but no bigger than a thumb. Then the parents said,

"He is just what we wished for, and we will love him very much," and they named him according to his stature, "Tom Thumb." And though they gave him plenty of nourishment, he grew no bigger, but remained exactly the same size as when he was first born; and he had very good faculties, and was very quick and prudent, so that all he did prospered.

One day his father made ready to go into the forest to cut wood, and he said, as if to himself,

"Now, I wish there was some one to bring the cart to meet me."

"O father," cried Tom Thumb, "I can bring the cart, let me alone for that, and in proper time, too!"

Then the father laughed, and said,

"How will you manage that? You are much too little to hold the reins."

"That has nothing to do with it, father; while my mother goes on with her spinning I will sit in the horse's ear and tell him where to go."

"Well," answered the father, "we will try it for once."

When it was time to set off, the mother went on spinning, after setting Tom Thumb in the horse's ear; and so he drove off, crying,

"Gee-up, gee-wo!"

So the horse went on quite as if his master were driving him, and drew the waggon along the right road to the wood.

Now it happened just as they turned a corner, and the little fellow was calling out "Gee-up!" that two strange men passed by.

"Look," said one of them, "how is this? There goes a waggon, and the driver is calling to the horse, and yet he is nowhere to be seen."

"It is very strange," said the other; "we will follow the waggon, and see where it belongs."

And the waggon went right through the wood, up to the place where the wood had been hewed. When Tom Thumb caught sight of his father, he cried out,

"Look, father, here am I with the waggon; now, take me down."

The father held the horse with his left hand, and with the right he lifted down his little son out of the horse's ear, and Tom Thumb sat down on a stump, quite happy and content. When the two strangers saw him they were struck dumb with wonder. At last one of them, taking the other aside, said to him, "Look here, the little chap would make our fortune if we were to show him in the town for money. Suppose we buy him."

So they went up to the woodcutter, and said,

"Sell the little man to us; we will take care he shall come to no harm."

"No," answered the father; "he is the apple of my eye, and not for all the money in the world would I sell him."

But Tom Thumb, when he heard what was going on, climbed up by his father's coat tails, and, perching himself on his shoulder, he whispered in his ear,

"Father, you might as well let me go. I will soon come back again."

Then the father gave him up to the two men for a large piece of money. They asked him where he would like to sit.

"Oh, put me on the brim of your hat," said he. "There I can walk about and view the country, and be in no danger of falling off."

So they did as he wished, and when Tom Thumb had taken leave of his father, they set off all together. And they travelled on until it grew dusk, and the little fellow asked to be set down a little while for a change, and after some difficulty they consented. So the man took him down from his hat, and set him in a field by the roadside, and he ran away directly, and, after creeping about among the furrows, he slipped suddenly into a mouse-hole, just what he was looking for.

"Good evening, my masters, you can go home without me!" cried he to them, laughing. They ran up and felt about with their sticks in the mouse-hole, but in vain. Tom Thumb crept farther and farther in, and as it was growing dark, they had to make the best of their way home, full of vexation, and with empty purses.

When Tom Thumb found they were gone, he crept out of his hiding-place underground.

"It is dangerous work groping about these holes in the darkness," said he; "I might easily break my neck."

But by good fortune he came upon an empty snail shell.

"That's all right," said he. "Now I can get safely through the night;" and he settled himself down in it. Before he had time to get to sleep, he heard two men pass by, and one was saying to the other,

"How can we manage to get hold of the rich parson's gold and silver?"

"I can tell you how," cried Tom Thumb.

"How is this?" said one of the thieves, quite frightened, "I hear some one speak!"

So they stood still and listened, and Tom Thumb spoke again.

"Take me with you; I will show you how to do it!"

"Where are you, then?" asked they.

"Look about on the ground and notice where the voice comes from," answered he.

At last they found him, and lifted him up.

"You little elf," said they, "how can you help us?"

"Look here," answered he, "I can easily creep between the iron bars of the parson's room and hand out to you whatever you would like to have."

"Very well," said they, "we will try what you can do."

So when they came to the parsonage-house, Tom Thumb crept into the room, but cried out with all his might,

"Will you have all that is here?" So the thieves were terrified, and said,

"Do speak more softly, lest any one should be awaked."

But Tom Thumb made as if he did not hear them, and cried out again,

"What would you like? will you have all that is here?" so that the cook, who was sleeping in a room hard by, heard it, and raised herself in bed and listened. The thieves, however, in their fear of being discovered, had run back part of the way, but they took courage again, thinking that it was only a jest of the little fellow's. So they came back and whispered to him to be serious, and to hand them out something.

Then Tom Thumb called out once more as loud as he could,

"Oh yes, I will give it all to you, only put out your hands."

Then the listening maid heard him distinctly that time, and jumped out of bed, and burst open the door. The thieves ran off as if the wild hunts-man were behind them; but the maid, as she could see nothing, went to fetch a light. And when she came back with one, Tom Thumb had taken himself off, without being seen by her, into the barn; and the maid, when she had looked in every hole and corner and found nothing, went back to bed at last, and thought that she must have been dreaming with her eyes and ears open.

So Tom Thumb crept among the hay, and found a comfortable nook to sleep in, where he intended to remain until it was day, and then to go home to his father and mother. But other things were to befall him; indeed, there is nothing but trouble and worry in this world! The maid got up at dawn of day to feed the cows. The first place she went to was the barn, where she took up an armful of hay, and it happened to be the very heap in which Tom Thumb lay asleep. And he was so fast asleep, that he was aware of nothing, and never waked until he was in the mouth of the cow, who had taken him up with the hay.

"Oh dear," cried he, "how is it that I have got into a mill!" but he soon found out where he was, and he had to be very careful not to get between the cow's teeth, and at last he had to descend into the cow's stomach.

"The windows were forgotten when this little room was built," said he, "and the sunshine cannot get in; there is no light to be had."

His quarters were in every way unpleasant to him, and, what was the worst, new hay was constantly coming in, and the space was being filled up. At last he cried out in his extremity, as loud as he could,

"No more hay for me! no more hay for me!"

The maid was then milking the cow, and as she heard a voice, but could see no one, and as it was the same voice that she had heard in the night, she was so frightened that she fell off her stool, and spilt the milk. Then she ran in great haste to her master, crying,

"Oh, master dear, the cow spoke!"

"You must be crazy," answered her master, and he went himself to the cow-house to see what was the matter. No sooner had he put his foot inside the door, than Tom Thumb cried out again,

"No more hay for me! no more hay for me!"

Then the parson himself was frightened, supposing that a bad spirit had entered into the cow, and he ordered her to be put to death. So she was killed, but the stomach, where Tom Thumb was lying, was thrown upon a dunghill. Tom Thumb had great trouble to work his way out of it, and he had just made a space big enough for his head to go through, when a new misfortune happened. A hungry wolf ran up and swallowed the whole stomach at one gulp. But Tom Thumb did not lose courage. "Perhaps," thought he, "the wolf will listen to reason," and he cried out from the inside of the wolf,

"My dear wolf, I can tell you where to get a splendid meal!"

"Where is it to be had?" asked the wolf.

"In such and such a house, and you must creep into it through the drain, and there you will find cakes and bacon and broth, as much as you can eat," and he described to him his father's house. The wolf needed not to be told twice. He squeezed himself through the drain in the night, and feasted in the store-room to his heart's content. When, at last, he was satisfied, he wanted to go away again, but he had become so big, that to creep the same way back was impossible. This Tom Thumb had reckoned upon, and began to make a terrible din inside the wolf, crying and calling as loud as he could.

"Will you be quiet?" said the wolf; "you will wake the folks up!"

"Look here," cried the little man, "you are very well satisfied, and now I will do something for my own enjoyment," and began again to make all the noise he could. At last the father and mother were awakened, and they ran to the room-door and peeped through the chink, and when they saw a wolf in occupation, they ran and fetched weapons—the man an axe, and the wife a scythe.

"Stay behind," said the man, as they entered the room; "when I have given him a blow, and it does not seem to have killed him, then you must cut at him with your scythe."

Then Tom Thumb heard his father's voice, and cried,

"Dear father, I am here in the wolf's inside."

Then the father called out full of joy,

"Thank heaven that we have found our dear child!" and told his wife to keep the scythe out of the way, lest Tom Thumb should be hurt with it. Then he drew near and struck the wolf such a blow on the head that he fell down dead; and then he fetched a knife and a pair of scissors, slit up the wolf's body, and let out the little fellow.

"Oh, what anxiety we have felt about you!" said the father.

"Yes, father, I have seen a good deal of the world, and I am very glad to breathe fresh air again."

"And where have you been all this time?" asked his father.

"Oh, I have been in a mouse-hole and a snail's shell, in a cow's stomach and a wolf's inside; now, I think, I will stay at home."

"And we will not part with you for all the king-doms of the world," cried the parents, as they kissed and hugged their dear little Tom Thumb. And they gave him something to eat and drink, and a new suit of clothes, as his old ones were soiled with travel.

Rapunzel

THERE ONCE LIVED a man and his wife, who had long wished for a child, but in vain. Now there was at the back of their house a little window which overlooked a beautiful garden full of the finest vegetables and flowers; but there was a high wall all round it, and no one ventured into it, for it belonged to a witch of great might, and of whom all the world was afraid. One day that the wife was standing at the window, and looking into the garden, she saw a bed filled with the finest rampion; and it looked so fresh and green that she began to wish for some; and at length she longed for it greatly. This went on for days, and as she knew she could not get the rampion, she pined away, and grew pale and miserable. Then the man was uneasy, and asked,

"What is the matter, dear wife?"

"Oh," answered she, "I shall die unless I can have some of that rampion to eat that grows in the garden at the back of our house." The man, who loved her very much, thought to himself,

"Rather than lose my wife I will get some rampion, cost what it will."

So in the twilight he climbed over the wall into the witch's garden, plucked hastily a handful of rampion and brought it to his wife. She made a salad of it at once, and ate of it to her heart's content. But she liked it so much, and it tasted so good, that the next day she longed for it thrice as much as she had done before; if she was to have any rest the man must climb over the wall once more. So he went in the twilight again; and as he was climbing back, he saw, all at once, the witch standing before him, and was terribly frightened, as she cried, with angry eyes,

"How dare you climb over into my garden like a thief, and steal my rampion! it shall be the worse for you!"

"Oh," answered he, "be merciful rather than just, I have only done it through necessity; for my wife saw your rampion out of the window, and became possessed with so great a longing that she would have died if she could not have had some to eat." Then the witch said,

"If it is all as you say you may have as much rampion as you like, on one condition—the child that will come into the world must be given to me. It shall go well with the child, and I will care for it like a mother."

In his distress of mind the man promised everything; and when the time came when the child was born the witch appeared, and, giving the child the name of Rapunzel (which is the same as rampion), she took it away with her.

Rapunzel was the most beautiful child in the world. When she was twelve years old the witch shut her up in a tower in the midst of a wood, and it had neither steps nor door, only a small window above. When the witch wished to be let in, she would stand below and would cry,

"Rapunzel, Rapunzel! let down your hair!"

Rapunzel had beautiful long hair that shone like gold. When she heard the voice of the witch she would undo the fastening of the upper window, unbind the plaits of her hair, and let it down twenty ells below, and the witch would climb up by it.

After they had lived thus a few years it happened that as the King's son was riding through the wood, he came to the tower; and as he drew near he heard a voice singing so sweetly that he stood still and listened. It was Rapunzel in her loneliness trying to pass away the time with sweet songs. The King's son wished to go in to her, and sought to find a door in the tower, but there was none. So he rode home, but the song had entered into his heart, and every day he went into the wood and listened to it. Once, as he was standing there under a tree, he saw the witch come up, and listened while she called out,

"O Rapunzel, Rapunzel! let down your hair."

Then he saw how Rapunzel let down her long tresses, and how the witch climbed up by it and went in to her, and he said to himself,

"Since that is the ladder I will climb it, and seek my fortune." And the next day, as soon as it began to grow dusk, he went to the tower and cried,

"O Rapunzel, Rapunzel! let down your hair."

And she let down her hair, and the King's son climbed up by it.

Rapunzel was greatly terrified when she saw that a man had come in to her, for she had never seen one before; but the King's son began speaking so kindly to her, and told how her singing had entered into his heart, so that he could have no peace until he had seen her herself. Then Rapunzel forgot her terror, and when he asked her to take him for her husband, and she saw that he was young and beautiful, she thought to herself,

"I certainly like him much better than old mother Gothel," and she put her hand into his hand, saying,

"I would willingly go with thee, but I do not know how I shall get out. When thou comest, bring each time a silken rope, and I will make a

"O Rapunzel, Rapunzel! let down your hair."

ladder, and when it is quite ready I will get down by it out of the tower, and thou shalt take me away on thy horse." They agreed that he should come to her every evening, as the old woman came in the day-time. So the witch knew nothing of all this until once Rapunzel said to her unwittingly,

"Mother Gothel, how is it that you climb up here so slowly, and the King's son is with me in a moment?"

"O wicked child," cried the witch, "what is this I hear! I thought I had hidden thee from all the world, and thou hast betrayed me!"

In her anger she seized Rapunzel by her beautiful hair, struck her several times with her left hand, and then grasping a pair of shears in her right—snip, snap—the beautiful locks lay on the ground. And she was so hard-hearted that she took Rapunzel and put her in a waste and desert place, where she lived in great woe and misery.

The same day on which she took Rapunzel away she went back to the tower in the evening and made fast the severed locks of hair to the window-hasp, and the King's son came and cried,

"Rapunzel, Rapunzel! let down your hair."

Then she let the hair down, and the King's son climbed up, but instead of his dearest Rapunzel he found the witch looking at him with wicked glittering eyes.

"Aha!" cried she, mocking him, "you came for your darling, but the sweet bird sits no longer in the nest, and sings no more; the cat has got her, and will scratch out your eyes as well! Rapunzel is lost to you, you will see her no more."

The King's son was beside himself with grief, and in his agony he sprang from the tower: he escaped with life, but the thorns on which he fell put out his eyes. Then he wandered blind through the wood, eating nothing but roots and berries, and doing nothing but lament and weep for the loss of his dearest wife.

So he wandered several years in misery until at last he came to the desert place where Rapunzel lived with her twin-children that she had borne, a boy and a girl. At first he heard a voice that he thought he knew, and when he reached the place from which it seemed to come Rapunzel knew him, and fell on his neck and wept. And when her tears touched his eyes they became clear again, and he could see with them as well as ever.

Then he took her to his kingdom, where he was received with great joy, and there they lived long and happily.